MY FRIEND
ROBOT!

The author would like to thank roboticist **Dr. Stefanie Tellex**, physicist and engineer **Dr. Adrian Parker** and carpenter **Nathanael Fedor** for reviewing the scientific accuracy of this book and for their help creating the endnotes.

Barefoot Books
2067 Massachusetts Ave
Cambridge, MA 02140

Barefoot Books
29/30 Fitzroy Square
London, W1T 6LQ

First published in Great Britain
by Barefoot Books, Ltd
and in the United States of America
by Barefoot Books, Inc in 2017
This paperback edition
first published in 2019
All rights reserved

Graphic design by
Sarah Soldano, Barefoot Books
Edited and art directed by
Kate DePalma, Barefoot Books
Reproduction by Bright Arts, Hong Kong
Printed in China on 100% acid-free paper
This book was typeset in Negrita Pro,
Sanchez and ITC Legacy Sans
The illustrations were prepared
in acrylics and digital collage

ISBN 978-1-78285-883-6

British Cataloguing-in-
Publication Data: a catalogue
record for this book is
available from the British Library

Library of Congress
Cataloging-in-Publication Data
is available upon request

7 9 8 6

For my Nick
— S. S.

**For my
whole family**
— H. S.

Go to *www.barefootbooks.com/myfriendrobot* to access
your audio singalong and video animation online.

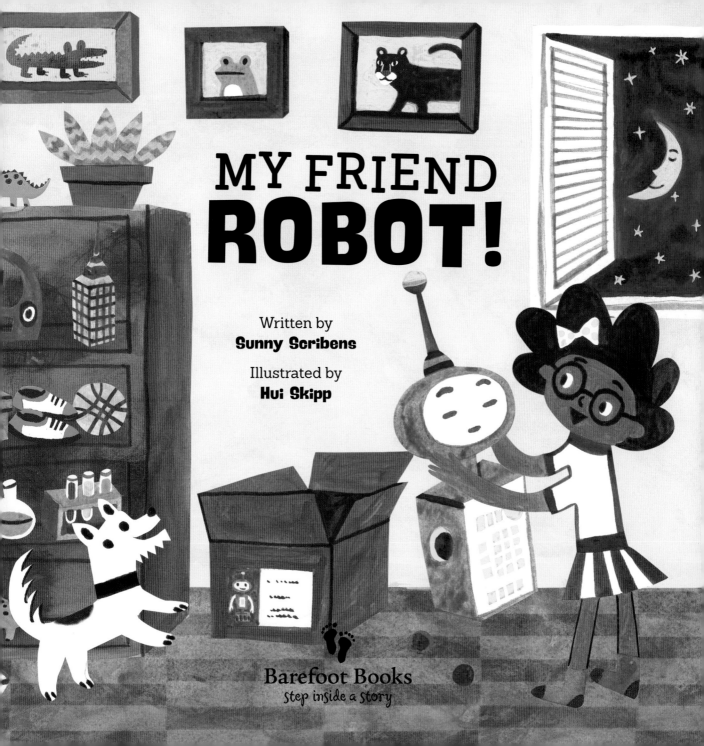

MY FRIEND
ROBOT!

Written by
Sunny Scribens

Illustrated by
Hui Skipp

Barefoot Books
Step inside a story

Who can help us build a house,
build a house, build a house?

Who can help us build a house?

My friend Robot!

First we need to split the wood,
split the wood, like we should.

Who can help us split the wood?
My friend Robot . . . *with a wedge!*

Now we've got to haul it out,
 haul it out — that's what it's about!

Who can help us haul it out?
My friend Robot ... *with a wagon!*

**Then we need to make the base,
make the base — hold it in place!**

Who can help us make the base?
My friend Robot . . . *with screws!*

Next it's time to build the walls,
build the walls — nice and tall!

Who can help us build the walls?
My friend Robot . . . *with a hammer!*

After that we raise the roof,
raise the roof — it's weatherproof!

Who can help us raise the roof?
My friend Robot . . . with a ladder!

**Last of all we hoist the flag,
hoist the flag — don't let it drag!**

Who can help us hoist the flag?
My friend Robot . . . *with a pulley!*

Puppy feels a little shy,
      little shy — oh, don't cry!

Who can help the little guy?
My friend Robot . . . *doesn't know.*

Pet him in a gentle way,
gentle way — it's been a long day.

Tell him it will be okay.
Like this, Robot!

Today has been a lot of fun,
lot of fun — thanks, everyone!

Now our tree house work is done.
Night night, Robot!

Simple Machines

When you think of a machine, you might think of something complicated, like an engine or a printer. But every machine is made up of what we call "simple machines" — basic devices that make work easier. The six most important simple machines are the wedge, wheel and axle, screw, lever, inclined plane and pulley.

Most of the tools we use every day are compound machines that combine two or more simple machines, including scissors (lever and wedge) and lawnmowers (wheel and axle, pulley and lever). How many simple and compound machines do the children in this story use to build their tree house? How many can you find in your own house?

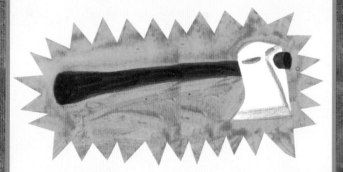

WEDGE

A wedge has a triangular shape. Some wedges, like axes, split things apart — the pointy end slides into a crack or crevice, and the larger end pushes it apart. Other wedges, like doorstops, hold things in place.

WHEEL AND AXLE

Smooth, round wheels roll over surfaces more easily than other shapes. If you attach a bar for the wheel to rotate around, that's called an axle. Axles allow wheels to connect to other objects and move big, bulky loads more easily.

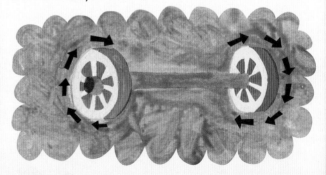

SCREW

If you look closely at a screw, you will notice a spiral groove that wraps around the outside. The groove allows you to drive a screw securely into wood and other materials by twisting in a circle, instead of applying force up and down like you do with a hammer and nail.

LEVER

A lever is a stick or a plank that helps you lift heavy things. The longer the lever, the more it helps. That's why the board of a seesaw is so long: it helps you lift the other person easily.

INCLINED PLANE

An inclined plane isn't a plane that flies, even though the terms sound alike! It's a slope that makes it easier to move from a lower place to a higher place, like a ramp or a ladder.

PULLEY

Add a rope to a wheel and you get a whole new machine: a pulley! You pull down on the rope of a pulley to hoist an object up. Pulling down feels easier than pulling up, because gravity helps you pull down.

What Can Robots Do?

?? ??

Robots can do all kinds of different tasks to help us. They can go into places that are dangerous for people, or do important work much faster and more easily than humans can.

Robots are created by robot scientists, who use mathematics, science and creativity to put together both the physical parts (hardware) and the computer code (software) that powers each robot.

Space Exploration

Robots have been used to explore space since the first satellites were launched in 1957. Voyager 1, a robot that was launched by the United States in 1977, was the first man-made object to leave our solar system, and it continues to send information back to the National Aeronautics and Space Administration of the United States (NASA) today.

Emergencies

Robots can go into places that might be dangerous for humans, so firefighters, police and other emergency services sometimes use robots when they need help or need to rescue someone. Robots are useful in many ways, from looking for people to spraying water for putting out fires.

Manufacturing

Robots are used to make many items, such as cars and planes. Robots are also used in warehouses to help the humans they work with pack boxes of books, toys and other things people buy.

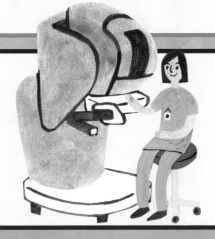

Health Care

Surgical robots help a surgeon make smaller cuts when they operate on a patient, which means the patient has less pain and heals faster. Robots cannot perform surgery by themselves — the surgeon controls the robot using a camera. Robots are also used to deliver medications in hospitals.

Housekeeeping

Robots can help with household chores like cleaning floors. Robot vacuums move around rooms on their own, sucking up dust as they go along. When the robot runs into something, it changes direction. It repeats this process until it has cleaned the entire floor. Which chores could a robot help you do?

Education and Play

Robots can be used to teach and entertain too. One of the most famous robotic toys is the Furby, which made history as the first robot widely purchased for home use when it was released in 1998. Do you play with robots at home or at school?

Programming Robots

Robots can do amazing things because of the way they are programmed. Robot scientists write computer programs that give robots instructions about what to do.

If you could program a robot to do anything, what would you choose?

If-Then Statements

The code that powers robots often uses if-then statements, like "**If** you run into an object, **then** stop moving" or "**If** you see a dog, **then** beep three times." The robots use the if-then statements as instructions for how to act.

Hardware and Software

Robots are made up of **hardware** and **software**. Hardware is the part of the robot you can see and feel, like motors and gears. Software is the information and instructions programmed into the robot. If the hardware is the robot's body parts, then the software is the thoughts in the robot's brain. Robot scientists usually create software by writing code (or **coding**) on a computer connected to the robot.

Play Scientist Says!

A game based on Simon Says

LEARN ABOUT PROGRAMMING

In this game, you can see what it's like to be a programmer . . . and what it's like to be a robot! The robots will perform actions that the robot scientist commands. You don't need a computer — just a friend (or a few!).

What You'll Need

- At least two players
- A safe space for moving around

How To Play

1. Choose one player to be the Robot Scientist. The other players will be the Robots.

2. The Scientist stands in front of the Robots and gives a command: **If** I _____, **then** you _____. For example, "**If** I clap my hands, **then** you stomp your feet."

3. If a Robot doesn't follow the command, then they are out! Continue giving new commands until there is only one Robot left. The last Robot standing becomes the Scientist in the next round!

Tips for Play

There's no limit to the actions you can try:

- Touch your nose
- Wiggle your hips
- Spin around
- Bark like a dog

Remember, everyone gets a turn to be the Scientist. Make sure you try having an adult play the Robot so you can make them do silly things.

WANT A BIGGER CHALLENGE?

Once you've got the basics, you can add a twist to keep the game exciting and challenging.

The Scientist can ask the Robots to perform actions in a sequence or order that they choose. For example, "If I shout 'Hooray!', then you jump up high, then wave your arms." Add another action each time until all of the Robots are out!

My Friend Robot!

Who can help us build a house, build a house, build a house?

(verse 2)

Who can help us build a house? My friend Ro - bot!